Ballet Bunnies

Millie's Birthday

By Swapna Reddy

Illustrated by Binny Talib

OXFORD
UNIVERSITY PRESS

Pod

Pod loves to build
things out of the
bits and bobs he
finds. He also loves
his tutu!

Trixie

Yawn! When
she's not dancing,
Trixie likes curling
up and having
a nice snooze.

For Ockie

OXFORD
UNIVERSITY PRESS

Great Clarendon Street, Oxford OX2 6DP

Oxford University Press is a department of the University of Oxford.
It furthers the University's objective of excellence in research, scholarship,
and education by publishing worldwide. Oxford is a registered trade mark
of Oxford University Press in the UK and in certain other countries

Database right Oxford University Press (maker)

First published 2020

British Library Cataloguing in Publication Data

Data available

ISBN:978-0-19-277487-3

1 3 5 7 9 10 8 6 4 2

Printed in China

Paper used in the production of this book is a natural,
recyclable product made from wood grown in sustainable forests.
The manufacturing process conforms to the environmental
regulations of the country of origin.

Chapter 1

'Wheeeeee!' Dolly whirled
around the empty ballet studio, spinning
forgotten ballet slippers across the floor
to Fifi, who dropped them in the lost
property box.

Millie smiled. It was the last day
of ballet class at Miss Luisa's School of

Dance before the holidays, and she had volunteered to tidy up the ballet studio until Mum came to pick her up. Miss Luisa had praised Millie for being such a good team player, but Millie had her own reasons to want to stay behind in the

empty studio alone. Four ballet-dancing, bunny-shaped reasons.

While Dolly pirouetted around, Pod helped Millie gather up the tutus the children had used during class, and Trixie, the fourth and tiniest of Millie's ballet-bunny friends, slept soundly in the warm pocket of Millie's hoody.

The Ballet Bunnies lived secretly in the school, and with no one but Millie in the studio they were free to dance (and sleep) there in the open.

'I'm going to miss you all during the holidays,' Millie said, as she held Trixie safely in her pocket.

'We're going to miss you too,' Fifi replied. She and Dolly pushed away the lost property box and hopped over to join Millie and Pod.

'What are you going to do over the holidays?' Dolly asked.

Millie blushed. 'Well, it's my birthday next week.'

Pod, Fifi, and Dolly leaped up high and landed on Millie's shoulders to give her the warmest birthday nuzzles.

'Why didn't you tell us?' Fifi exclaimed. 'Are you having a big party?'

Millie nodded. 'Mum is throwing me a big, ballet birthday party next week,' she said.

'How exciting,' Dolly squealed.

Pod looked thoughtfully at Millie as Dolly squeaked excitedly about how much she loved parties.

'Is everything OK, Millie?' Pod asked, gently.

Millie sighed. 'I was really excited

when Mum told me about the party, but now I'm a bit worried about so many people coming to our house.'

'But that's the best bit!' Dolly said. 'All those people are there to celebrate *you*.'

The bunnies hopped off Millie's shoulders as she slumped down to the ground and they gathered close around her.

'I get a funny, whirly feeling in my tummy when I think about everyone coming to the party,' said Mille. 'It feels like the inside of me is spinning too fast on a ride at the fairground.'

Fifi and Dolly fell silent as Pod hopped even closer. 'I understand, Millie,' he said. 'Sometimes all the noise and attention can feel a bit overwhelming.'

Millie gazed down at the little bunny and scooped him up. 'I wish you could

all come home with me for the holidays,'
she said. 'I would feel much better about
the party if you bunnies were there.'

'I wish we could, too,' Fifi agreed.

Millie thought for a moment. 'Well, why can't you?' She jumped up, her eyes bright and excited. 'You could stay in my room and we could dance and play all day. And then you could come to my party, too.'

'Yes!' Dolly shrieked. 'This is a brilliant plan.'

'Oh, bunny fluff,' Fifi said, slowly. 'What if someone like Millie's mum sees us? Do you think we can stay hidden for that long?'

Before Millie could answer, Trixie's tiny face poked out from Millie's pocket.

'Of course we can!'
she said.

Chapter 2

Taking the bunnies home in her bag was going to be tricky. They were far too heavy for Millie to be able to skip all the way home the way she usually did with Mum. And if she didn't skip, Mum might start asking questions.

So Millie kept Trixie tucked up away

in her pocket, while Dolly snuck into Millie's bag.

'We can follow behind and keep out of sight,' Pod and Fifi had agreed.

Millie kept Mum as distracted as possible on the way home, asking her questions about her day and sharing stories from the last ballet class.

Just a few doors away from their house, Mum stopped suddenly and spun round to look behind Millie, who turned to see that Fifi and Pod must have darted behind a nearby tree trunk to stand as still as statues.

'Mum?' Millie started. She bounced
nervously from foot to foot and held on
to Trixie a little bit tighter.

Mum shook her head and turned
back. 'I thought someone was behind us,'
she said, confused, before skipping on
beside Millie all the way to their front
door.

⊙ ✳ ⊙

'That was close!' Dolly said as she
scrambled out of Millie's bag the
moment the four bunnies were safely
in Millie's bedroom.

Pod picked out a leaf from his fur. 'I
told you we should have hidden behind

that postbox, Fifi.'

'Oh, bunny fluff,' Fifi
said, dismissively. 'We're
all here now, aren't we?'

She bounced up
and down on Millie's
bed, before lying back
in the soft sheets. 'This
is going to be the best
bunny holiday ever,'
she said, grinning at the
others.

Trixie yawned and her nose twitched as Millie placed her carefully down by her musical jewellery box. The little bunny popped open the lid to see the tiny ballerina inside begin to rotate to the tune from the box. Fifi, Pod, and Dolly giggled with glee, and together all four bunnies pirouetted around the box in time with the twinkly melody.

'Oh!' Fifi gasped. 'Who is *that*?'

She stood motionless with one paw pointing in front of her.

Millie smiled and picked up the beautiful ballerina doll Fifi was gawping at. The china doll was dressed in a pink-silk ballet dress and had miniature ivory ballet slippers on her feet. Her dark hair was pulled back in a bun and yellow satin flowers were pinned behind her ear.

Carefully holding the doll, Millie sat down on her bed to show it to the bunnies.

'She was my Granny's when she was a little girl,' Millie said. 'Granny named her Sylvie after a famous dancer she knew.'

Millie reached up to a shelf above her bed and pulled down a little blue hat with bunny ears made out of paper.

'I made this for Sylvie,' she said as she placed the hat on Sylvie's head.

'Now she looks like one of us,' Fifi exclaimed.

Dolly hopped closer and gently ruffled the hem of Sylvie's dress. As the dress tumbled back into place, the pink fabric shimmered.

'She's so special,' Dolly whispered.

'She's the most special thing I have.'

29

Millie smiled. But her smile quickly gave way to a frown. 'Mum is always telling me to be more careful with Sylvie. I keep leaving her around the house, but really she needs to stay where she will be safe.'

Millie then put Sylvie back on her shelf.

'I know,' Dolly said. 'Let's show Sylvie our *pliés*,'

Millie lined up alongside the bunnies as they turned out their heels and curtseyed into a *plié*.

'And now, *relevé*,' Dolly said, sounding just like Miss Luisa, the ballet teacher.

Millie and the bunnies laughed but rose up on their tiptoes just as Dolly had asked.

'And now *disco pirouettes*!' Dolly cried.

Millie fell back onto her bed, laughing really hard as Dolly wiggled her bottom and twirled in circles.

'*What exactly is going on in here?*'

Chapter 3

Millie spun round to see
Mum in the doorway.

'Mum!'

'Well?' Mum demanded.

'I . . .' Millie stammered. 'I can
explain, Mum.'

Millie could feel her heart pounding

hard in her chest. She couldn't believe it.
The bunnies had been discovered *already*.

Perhaps Mum would understand if
she got to know the Ballet Bunnies? she
thought. In any case, Millie had no choice
now but to introduce them. She turned to
pick up her friends.

But they had all disappeared!

Millie's eyes darted around her room.
Where had they gone?

'Well?' Mum said, tapping her foot.

Millie was just going to have to tell
Mum the truth.

She opened her mouth to explain, but
Mum interrupted her.

'Are you going to explain why you were playing *without* me?' Mum said. But a smile broke across her face.

Millie was confused. Had Mum really not seen Dolly, Fifi, Trixie, and Pod?

Mum plonked down on Millie's bed and picked up a teddy bear. 'So, what are we playing?'

'I *was* playing hide and seek with my toys,' Millie said quickly, distracted as she searched the room for the bunnies.

They weren't in the toybox. They weren't under her pillow. They weren't hidden between her books. And they weren't burrowed in her rolls of ribbons.

Suddenly, the tiniest of tiny twitches caught her eye. There, in amongst her pile of teddy bears, were all the bunnies. One was wearing a borrowed teddy hat, one had on a pair of teddy spectacles, another was wrapped in a teddy scarf, and the fourth bunny was snoozing on top of a fluffy unicorn.

Millie put her hand over her mouth to stop herself from laughing.

'It's almost time for dinner, so I'm not sure we can play a *whole* game of hide and seek,' Mum said. 'How about we play after dinner?'

Millie nodded and threw herself into

Mum's arms to shield the bunnies from view.

'I can't believe you are going to be a whole year older next week.' Mum said, kissing Millie on the forehead. 'Are you still excited about your party?'

Millie sat in Mum's lap, her worries about the party coming back. Then her foot brushed a teddy bear on the floor and she remembered her four little bunny friends, who'd promised to help her through the next week.

'Yes, Mum.' She nodded. 'I can't wait for the party.'

Mum smiled, and as soon as she'd headed back downstairs, Dolly, Fifi, Pod, and Trixie hopped out of their hiding spots amongst the bears.

'Can we still come to your party?' Dolly asked, hopefully.

'Ooh, I hope so!' Fifi added.

Millie scooped up Pod and grinned at the others.

'I couldn't have a party without all of you!' she said.

Chapter 4

The next week was filled with fun and dancing. One day, Millie took the bunnies for a cycle ride, tucking them into the basket on the front of her bike. Another day, they all pirouetted around the garden and did the conga across her bedroom. And every bedtime

Millie read Fifi, Dolly, Pod, and Trixie stories about ballerina ponies and tap-dancing kangaroos.

The bunnies had been brilliant at keeping out of sight. Whenever Millie's mum appeared they would either dart behind Millie's stash of comics or burrow under the duvet in the nick of time. Trixie even managed to hide on top of one of Mum's fluffy slippers without Mum noticing!

With all the holiday fun she was having, Millie hadn't had a chance to think about how nervous she was about her party. But now, as she gazed around

the garden and at the long table dressed
in its blue polka-dot cloth and laden
with star-shaped sandwiches, pink wafer
biscuits, purple fairy cakes with sprinkles,
and a strawberry-flavoured cake topped
with ballet shoes made of pink icing,
the whirling feeling in her tummy had
returned.

'Millie,' Dolly said as she bounded across the garden. 'Follow me.'

Millie caught a glimpse of Dolly's golden fur whipping under the long tablecloth that reached down to the grass. She dropped down and crawled under the table to join her friend.

'Oh, Dolly!' Millie gasped.

Fifi, Pod, Trixie, and Dolly had created a bunny den under the table of

food. In one corner, there were fairy lights and tiny cushions from Millie's doll's house; in another, there was an empty egg carton which had been painted in blue polka dots and laden with snacks for the bunnies. It was just like the table they were sitting under.

'What's this?' Millie asked, as she looked inside a shoebox full of old wrapping paper.

'That's where we hide in case someone looks under the table,' Fifi explained.

'Millie!' a voice called from the house.

'I've got to go,' Millie said, hugging each bunny in turn.

'Have fun!' Dolly squealed, as party music started to play in the garden.

Millie clambered out from under the table and dusted off her dress. Mum had bought the frock especially for the party and it was covered in tiny sparkly prints of ballet shoes.

'Millie, let's play!' a group of her friends from school called out.

She hurried over to find that Mum had set up a game of Pin the Tutu on the Ballerina. It was Millie's turn. Mum tied a thick satin ribbon over Millie's eyes so she couldn't see and spun her round. Millie clutched the pin attached to the tutu and held out her arms to try and feel for the picture of the ballerina.

'Go, Millie, go!' her friends cheered.

Millie grinned as she poked the pin through where she thought the tutu should be and then whipped off her blindfold, only to find that she'd pinned it to the ballerina's head.

She and her friends fell about

laughing when Mum took her turn and pinned the tutu to the collar of Aunty May's cardigan that was hanging off the back of a chair.

'Time for Musical Statues!' Mum called out. 'And there are prizes for whoever holds the best ballerina poses.'

Millie giggled as her friends groaned. There was only person who could possibly win: ballet-mad Millie.

Chapter 5

As the music stopped,

everyone froze in their best ballerina poses. Millie stood high on her tiptoes in the *relevé* position that she had practised with Dolly earlier that week.

And that's when she saw Sylvie! Granny's china doll was being dragged

across the garden by Adam, her
friend Samira's little brother.

Oh, no, thought Millie. She
remembered she'd been playing with
Sylvie again this morning in the living
room, while Mum was busy getting the
party ready. She had meant to put her
safely back on the shelf
in her bedroom, but
she'd forgotten!

Millie broke out of her pose and ran towards Sylvie, but then stopped. Mum always said she should share her toys, especially with younger children. It was the kind thing to do.

Sylvie's neat bun began to unravel as Adam combed his fingers through her silky hair.

Millie wrung her hands. She wanted to grab Sylvie off Adam, but she didn't want to upset him. Her stomach churned so hard she felt like she had to hold it in place. She had to find Mum. Mum would know what to do.

Millie scoured the garden. It suddenly

felt far too loud and far too full of people.
She looked back at Adam who was still
gripping Sylvie much too tight. Where
was Mum?

Millie hurried across the lawn,
squeezing through the group of parents.
Musical Statues had just finished as
Millie ran past her friends, searching
for Mum.

There she was! But now Mum was with a group of grown-ups, and she looked extremely busy pouring out lemonade into tumblers for everyone.

Millie blinked hard as she felt tears in her eyes. She needed someone to help her.

And then she remembered the four little bunnies, hiding under a table.

Chapter 6

'Adam has Sylvie!' Millie cried as she dove under the tablecloth.

Fifi quickly poked her head out from under the table. 'Millie's right,' she confirmed.

'I need to get her back,' Millie sobbed. 'She's too delicate to be played

with but I don't want to upset Adam,
and Mum is very busy with the party.'

Pod and Trixie nuzzled into Millie's
wet cheeks as she cried into her party
dress.

'Don't worry, Millie,' Dolly said. 'I have a plan.'

Millie and the other bunnies looked over at Dolly, who had whipped off her tutu and was rocking back on her hind legs.

'Oh, *bunny fluff,*' Fifi gasped.

'What are you doing, Dolly?' Millie cried.

'I'm going full-on rabbit,' Dolly said, and bounded out from under the table.

Millie sprang out in time to see Dolly jump across the lawn and into full view of everyone at the party.

'Dolly!' Millie screeched.

Everyone turned to look at her.

'Bunny!' Adam screeched back.

Now everyone turned to look at him.

He dropped Sylvie and chased after
Dolly, who decided to take the scenic
route around the garden and hopped a
full circuit through all the guests' legs
and over the garden gnomes before
darting out of sight across Mum's
vegetable patch.

Millie used the distraction to rescue
Sylvie. She ran towards the doll and
bundled her up quickly, holding her close
to her chest.

She smoothed and tidied Sylvie's hair

as she made sure her favourite doll wasn't damaged. Her chest felt heavy and her mouth as dry as sand as she checked Sylvie's arms and legs, and then her silk dress and slippers.

Sylvie was in good condition. She had been saved just in time, thanks to Dolly's plan. Still, Millie couldn't stop the heavy tears rolling down her cheeks as she hugged her doll tight and thought of the huge risk Dolly had taken to help her.

Chapter 7

As the bunny commotion
in the garden died down, Millie slid back
under the table and into the bunnies' den.

Fifi had gone to find Dolly, leaving
Pod and Trixie alone in the den when
Millie joined them.

'Oh, Millie,' Trixie said, as she

snuggled against Millie's arm. 'At least Sylvie is OK.'

'But she might not have been,' Millie sobbed, her shoulders slumped forward. 'And it would've been all my fault. Mum is always telling me to put her away and I always forget.'

'Luckily, Dolly saved the day,' Pod said.

'But who knows what could've happened to Dolly!' Millie wept. 'She could have been hurt trying to help me.'

'But she wasn't,' Pod reassured her. 'And by the looks of it, she had the time of her life running around your party.'

Millie brushed away her tears with her sleeve, but she couldn't get rid of the horrible, whirling feeling inside that was bubbling up from her tummy.

She hung her head low. 'I wish I'd never had a party.'

Pod gazed up at Millie, his eyes full of kindness.

'I mean it,' Millie said, trying to blink back more tears. 'I could never have forgiven myself if something had happened to Dolly or Sylvie.'

Millie gently picked up Sylvie and straightened her pink ballet dress. She untied Sylvie's hair and combed her fingers through it before carefully twisting it back into a bun. Then she pinned back the little yellow satin flowers behind Sylvie's ear. Trixie helped straighten up Sylvie's slippers as Pod jumped onto Millie's shoulder and dabbed at her tear-stained cheeks with his paws.

'I just wish everyone would go home now,' Millie whispered. 'The party is too loud and there are too many people here. It's all too much.'

She looked around the den and at the warm lights and cushions the bunnies had placed in the soft grass. Under the table, away from the noise and close to Pod and Trixie, Millie felt safe.

'I'm going to stay here until everyone goes home,' she announced. 'I'm not moving.'

Chapter 8

'You can stay here as long
as you want, Millie,' Trixie told her.

'And it's OK to feel upset,' Pod said.

'Really?' Millie sniffed.

'Of course,' Pod said. 'I find noise and
crowds sometimes upset me, too. I get
a horrible feeling in my tummy and my

chest feels tight.'

'That's exactly how I feel,' Millie exclaimed.

'I have a good trick that helps me during those times,' Pod said. 'I can teach it to you if you want?'

Millie nodded eagerly and sat down cross-legged with the bunnies.

'First, you need to shut your eyes,' Pod said, as he closed his.

Millie and Trixie shut their eyes too.

'Now, you need to take some deep breaths in and out,' Pod said. 'Imagine you are smelling a beautiful flower as you breathe in. Then imagine you are blowing

away dandelion seeds as you breathe out.'

Millie took a deep breath in. And then let the breath out.

She did it a few times until she could almost smell the honeysuckle on the outside of her house. As she breathed out she imagined she was in a meadow, blowing dandelion seeds, with the warm sun on her face and the birds tweeting in the trees above.

With every breath in and out, the sound of the party quietened and Millie could feel the tightness in her chest and the whirling in her tummy melt away.

After five breaths, she opened her eyes and saw Pod and Trixie do the same.

'This final part is the most important bit,' Pod said. 'Find someone you love and give them a cuddle.'

Millie gathered up Trixie and Pod and held them close.

'Thank you, Pod,' Millie said. 'I feel a

lot better.'

She kissed the little bunnies on their heads and stroked their long ears before placing them back on the ground.

'Now that you're here,' Trixie started. 'You can join in *our* party games.'

Millie laughed and crawled after Trixie who led her to the far end of the table. There, strung up on the table leg was a picture of a bunny. Trixie handed Millie a cotton ball with a small tack on the end.

'We're playing Pin the Tail on the Bunny,' Trixie said, jumping with glee. 'It's your turn now, Millie.'

Millie shut her eyes and reached out,
before accidently tacking the tail on the
nose of the bunny. Pod and Trixie rolled
about on the grass giggling at the fluffy-

nosed bunny picture.

'We played a game just like this,' Millie laughed. 'But we had to place the tutu on the ballerina and Mum pinned it to Aunty May's cardigan.'

The bunnies giggled again. 'That sounds like so much fun,' Trixie said.

'It was,' Millie agreed.

'What else did you play?' Pod asked.

'We had a game of Musical Statues but we had to pose as ballerinas when the music stopped,' Millie said. 'I stopped in *relevé*,' she added, proudly.

'I bet you won that game,' Pod said.

Millie's smile faded to a frown.

'That's when I saw Samira's little brother with Sylvie.'

Trixie placed her paw on Millie's hand. 'It sounded like a wonderful party up until then.'

'It was,' Millie admitted. 'I was having lots of fun.'

She poked her head out from under the tablecloth and saw her friends playing a dancing game on the lawn.

'It's OK to go back out there if you want to,' Pod encouraged her.

Seeing her friends dance made Millie realize how much fun her party had been, and now Sylvie was safely back

with her she really did want
to dance, too.

Millie sat up and crawled to the
edge of the table. 'I think I will go back,'
she said, bravely. 'I'll put Sylvie back
upstairs in my bedroom, and then I'll go
and have more fun.'

'Go, Millie, go!' Pod and Trixie
cheered.

Millie held Sylvie close and waved
at the bunnies as scrambled out from
under the table and waved to her
friends.

Chapter 9

Mum saw off the last of the guests as Millie handed out the remaining party bags. Mum had filled each bag with a little wooden ballet doll and matching hairbands.

As soon as everyone left, Millie rushed over to the bunny den and lifted the tablecloth. She hadn't seen Dolly since the commotion and she was a little worried that she might not have made it back yet.

But the den was empty of *all* the bunnies. Millie looked in the shoebox, too, but they weren't in there.

Millie hurried upstairs to look for her friends, but her bedroom was empty.

There were no bunnies on the bookshelf, nor were there any of her friends in the teddy pile.

And then the duvet slipped back.

'Happy Birthday, Millie!' Trixie, Pod, Dolly, and Fifi yelled, as they jumped out from under the bedsheets.

Happy birthday!

'You were hiding!' Millie exclaimed, gathering them up in a huge cuddle.

'Did you see me? Did you see me?' Dolly said, as she wiggled her bottom excitedly. 'I ran across the *whole* garden!'

'You did,' Millie laughed. 'And you saved Sylvie.'

Millie placed a big kiss on Dolly's head as the little bunny jumped out of her arms and sprang around the bedroom recreating her daring garden run.

'Did you enjoy the rest of your party?' Pod asked Millie.

Millie nodded. 'I had the best time,' she said. 'And I've made plans for the rest

of the holidays to see all my friends from
the party.'

'That sounds wonderful,' Fifi said.

'It certainly does,' Dolly agreed. 'And
it also sounds like that's *our* cue to head
back to Miss Luisa's School of Dance.'

'Already?' Millie said, a little disappointed.

'You've got lots of fun with your friends to look forward to,' Dolly said.

Millie smiled. Dolly was right.

She waved the bunnies off as they climbed out of her window and hopped across the garden towards the dance school.

And then Millie smiled at Sylvie who was back on her shelf, safe from harm and far away from little brothers.

Basic ballet moves

First position

Second position

Third
position

Fourth
position

Fifth position

How to make bunny ears!

You will need:

- A spare plastic Alice band
- Card
- Scissors
- Crayons/glitter/anything you like for decoration
- Glue/sticky tape

1 Draw your bunny ears on the card. Make them a little bit longer than you want them to be.

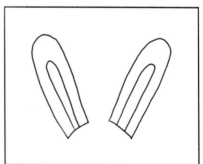

2 Decorate your ears any way you like!

3 Once your decorated ears are dry, cut them out.

4 Fold the bottom of the ears around the Alice band, and use sticky tape or glue to secure.

5 Enjoy being a bunny!

About the author

Award-winning author
Swapna Reddy, who also
writes as Swapna Haddow,
lives in New Zealand with
her husband and son and
their dog, Archie.

If she wasn't writing books,
she would love to run a
detective agency or wash
windows because she's
very nosy.

About the illustrator

Binny Talib is a Sydney based illustrator who loves to create wallpaper, branding, children's books, editorial, packaging and anything else she can draw all over.

Binny recently returned from living in awesome Hong Kong and now works happily on beautiful Sydney harbour with other lovely creative folks, drinking copious amounts of dandelion tea, and is inspired by Jasper her rescue cat.

If you enjoyed this adventure, you might also like . . .

Kitty
and the
Twilight Trouble

Girl by day. Cat by night. Ready for adventure.
Written by Paula Harrison · *Illustrated by* Jenny Løvlie

Written by Gill Lewis

Willow Wildthing
and the
Swamp Monster

Illustrated by Rebecca Bagley

ISADORA MOON
Has a Birthday

Half vampire, half fairy, totally unique!
Harriet Muncaster

From the world of ISADORA MOON
MIRABELLE
Gets up to Mischief

Half witch, half fairy, totally naughty!
Harriet Muncaster